The Twelve Days of
CHRISTMAS

ALISON JAY

Alfred A. Knopf · New York

On the first
day of Christmas,
my true love gave to me . . .

a partridge in a pear tree.

On the second day of Christmas, my true love gave to me . . .

two turtle doves
and a partridge in a pear tree.

*

On the third day of Christmas, my true love gave to me . . .

three French hens,
two turtle doves
and a partridge in a pear tree.

On the fourth day of Christmas, my true love gave to me . . .

four calling birds,
three French hens,
two turtle doves
and a partridge in a pear tree.

*

On the fifth day of Christmas, my true love gave to me . . .

five gold rings.

four calling birds,
three French hens,
two turtle doves
and a partridge in a pear tree.

*

On the sixth day of Christmas,
my true love gave to me . . .

six geese a-laying,
five gold rings,
four calling birds,
three French hens,
two turtle doves
and a partridge in a pear tree.

On the seventh day of Christmas, my true love gave to me . . .

seven swans a-swimming,
six geese a-laying,
five gold rings,
four calling birds,
three French hens,
two turtle doves
and a partridge in a pear tree.

*

On the eighth day of Christmas,
my true love gave to me . . .

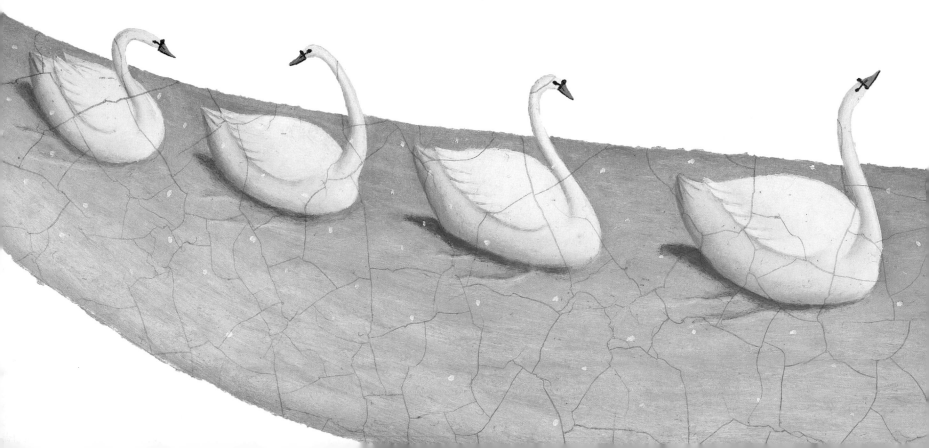

eight maids a-milking,
seven swans a-swimming,
six geese a-laying,
five gold rings,
four calling birds,
three French hens,
two turtle doves
and a partridge in a pear tree.

On the ninth day of Christmas, my true love gave to me . . .

nine drummers drumming,
eight maids a-milking,
seven swans a-swimming,
six geese a-laying,
five gold rings,
four calling birds,
three French hens,
two turtle doves
and a partridge in a pear tree.

On the tenth day of Christmas,
my true love gave to me . . .

ten ladies dancing,
nine drummers drumming,
eight maids a-milking,
seven swans a-swimming,
six geese a-laying,
five gold rings,
four calling birds,
three French hens,
two turtle doves
and a partridge in a pear tree.

On the eleventh day of Christmas,
my true love gave to me . . .

eleven pipers piping,
ten ladies dancing,
nine drummers drumming,
eight maids a-milking,
seven swans a-swimming,
six geese a-laying,
five gold rings,
four calling birds,
three French hens,
two turtle doves
and a partridge in a pear tree.

On the twelfth day of Christmas, my true love gave to me . . .

twelve lords a-leaping, eleven pipers piping, ten ladies dancing,

nine drummers drumming, eight maids a-milking,

four calling birds, three French hens, two turtle doves . . . .

seven swans a-swimming, six geese a-laying, five gold rings,

and a partridge
in a pear tree.

For leaping-lord Simon, love from the dancing goose —A.J.

THIS IS A BORZOI BOOK PUBLISHED BY ALFRED A. KNOPF

Jacket art and interior illustrations copyright © 2014 by Alison Jay

All rights reserved. Published in the United States by Alfred A. Knopf, an imprint of Random House Children's Books, a division of Random House LLC, a Penguin Random House Company, New York. Originally published in hardcover by Templar Publishing, UK, in 2014.

Knopf, Borzoi Books, and the colophon are registered trademarks of Random House LLC.

Visit us on the Web! randomhousekids.com

Educators and librarians, for a variety of teaching tools, visit us at RHTeachersLibrarians.com

The Library of Congress Cataloging-in-Publication Data is available upon request.

ISBN 978-0-553-49661-1 (trade) — ISBN 978-0-553-49662-8 (lib. bdg.) — ISBN 978-0-553-49663-5 (ebook)

The illustrations in this book were created using alkyd paint and crackle varnish on thick cartridge paper.

Designed by Janie Louise Hunt

MANUFACTURED IN CHINA
October 2015
10 9 8 7 6 5 4 3 2 1

First American Edition

Random House Children's Books supports the First Amendment and celebrates the right to read.